TALES FROM AROUND THE WORLD

A Classic Collection

First published in this edition 2008
First published in Great Britain in 2005 by Zero To Ten Limited
2A Portman Mansions, Chiltern Street, London W1U 6NR

This edition © 2008 Zero To Ten Ltd
© Larousse 2004

British Library Cataloguing in Publication Data:
Tales from around the world
1. Tales - Juvenile literature
2. 398.2

9781840895353
Printed in Malaysia

TALES FROM AROUND THE WORLD

A Classic Collection

ZERO TO TEN

CONTENTS

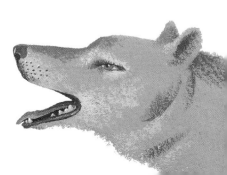

ALADDIN
AND THE MAGIC LAMP

Once in a distant city of Arabia, there was a poor tailor called Mustapha. He had a thirteen year-old son named Aladdin, and Mustapha wished to teach him the family business. However Aladdin had no interest in cutting and sewing cloth, and spent all his time playing about the streets with his friends. Mustapha tried to get Aladdin to pay attention, but every time he turned his back, Aladdin was out with his friends. Eventually, Mustapha fell ill from the stresses of work and died. Aladdin's mother sold the business and spun cotton for a living. This didn't worry Aladdin, who continued to waste his days round the streets of the city. However, this all changed when Aladdin was fifteen years old.

It was a beautiful day and, as usual, Aladdin was playing with his friends. A powerful and devious magician from Maghreb watched the boys. After asking some passers-by who the silliest of the boys was, the magician's eyes lit up, and he went up to Aladdin and said:

"Say, aren't you Mustapha the tailor's boy?"

"That's right," replied Aladdin, "but my father has been dead for these last two years."

"My boy, what are you telling me?" asked the magician, breaking down in tears. "My brother, dead? And after I have travelled all this way."

Eventually he stopped crying and looked at Aladdin for a moment.

"You are my only consolation on this terrible day," said the magician. "A man is not dead if he has family. Why don't you and your mother come and live with me? What do you say?" With that he slipped ten gold coins into Aladdin's hand.

Aladdin was won over and agreed to the stranger's suggestion. Promising to meet him the next day, Aladdin ran home with the gold and the good news. His mother was surprised by the story for, truth be told, her husband had never mentioned that he had a brother; but Aladdin was so enthusiastic that she allowed herself to get carried along with it all.

The next day the magician arrived loaded with wine and fruits. At dinner the magician spoke about his dead brother and his moving speech touched the heart of Aladdin's mother. Turning to Aladdin, the magician asked: "Tell me, how do you spend your days?"

The question embarrassed the boy, and he hung his head in silence.

"Aladdin is a lazy boy, who wastes his time with his friends," explained his mother. "His dear father tried to teach him the trade, but it went in one ear and out the other. Now he acts like he hasn't a care in the world, while I spin cotton to make ends meet."

The magician frowned:

"Oh my nephew," he said, "I am annoyed to hear this! Everyone must have a trade of some sort. If your father's was not to your taste, then you must pick another – there are plenty to choose from. Think about it and decide what you want to do."

Aladdin stayed quiet, because he didn't really want to learn anything.

"Wouldn't you like to become a rich merchant and deal in fine fabrics?" asked the magician. "That's what I suggest you should do; then you could provide for yourself and your mother."

It sounded like a fantastic idea. Fabric merchants were respected members of society and Aladdin had long admired their fine clothes. He readily accepted the magician's proposal.

"In which case," said the magician, "I will return tomorrow with some decent clothes for you and present you to the merchants of the city."

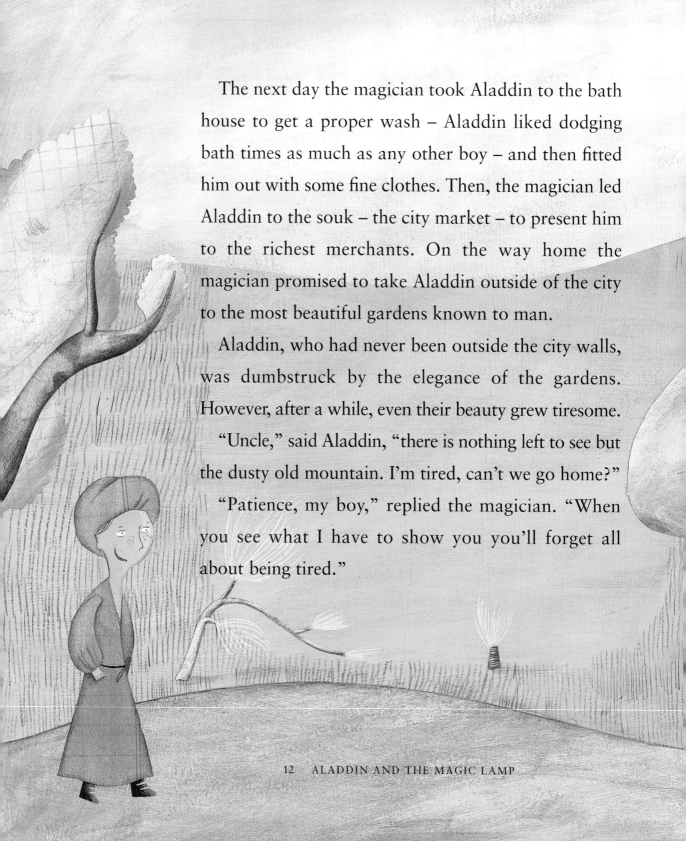

The next day the magician took Aladdin to the bath house to get a proper wash – Aladdin liked dodging bath times as much as any other boy – and then fitted him out with some fine clothes. Then, the magician led Aladdin to the souk – the city market – to present him to the richest merchants. On the way home the magician promised to take Aladdin outside of the city to the most beautiful gardens known to man.

Aladdin, who had never been outside the city walls, was dumbstruck by the elegance of the gardens. However, after a while, even their beauty grew tiresome.

"Uncle," said Aladdin, "there is nothing left to see but the dusty old mountain. I'm tired, can't we go home?"

"Patience, my boy," replied the magician. "When you see what I have to show you you'll forget all about being tired."

The pair trekked on until they arrived at a small valley in the middle of the desert. The magician lit a fire, threw a pinch of incense on it and chanted a magic spell. Immediately the valley began to shake, rocks split in half and the ground parted to reveal a metal trapdoor. Aladdin was at first petrified with fear, then turned to run but was knocked to the ground by a hard slap. The magician looked at him and said softly:

"My boy," said the magician, "I'm sorry that I hit you, but it is for your own good. You were about to run and an immense treasure waits down there. Just say the name of your father and your grandfather to open the door."

Aladdin obeyed: "I am Aladdin, son of Mustapha the tailor, who was the son of Ali the tailor." The door opened.

"Now," said the magician. "Go down there, through the garden, and look for a lamp. Take care not to touch anything else or it will mean instant death. When you bring back the lamp you may collect as many fruits as you like. Take this ring – it may help you if anything bad happens."

Aladdin went down the stairs and found himself in a garden packed with the most luxuriant fruit trees. There were chests filled with precious stones and jars overflowing with money. Eventually he found the lamp and took it back to the magician. On the way he collected some fruits, which to his surprise, looked like glass balls. He crammed so many in his clothes that he needed help to climb the stairs.

"Uncle," cried Aladdin, "help me climb out!"

"Throw me the lamp first," replied the magician.

Aladdin was young but he wasn't stupid, so he refused to throw the lamp up. The magician flew into a rage, screaming, "You insolent wretch, how dare you disobey me? You'll pay for this with your life!"

He shouted some magic words and the trap door swung shut and the ground sealed up again, trapping Aladdin in the underground garden. In truth, the magician had never intended that Aladdin would leave that place, but now the magician had also lost the lamp he had been seeking for many years.

Aladdin hammered at the door but it remained locked – he was buried alive. He cried out for help for the rest of the day, but no one came to his aid. Aladdin fell to his knees and prayed to Allah for help. While he prayed he wrung his hands together, but without realising it, he was also rubbing the ring the magician had given him. Immediately a huge creature appeared – it was a genie and he filled the space in front of Aladdin. Looking down at the boy, the genie said:

"I am the genie of the ring. Your wish is my command."

Aladdin was struck dumb, but he finally summoned up the courage to ask the genie to help him escape. Immediately the ground above them cracked open. Aladdin headed straight home to the welcoming arms of his mother. Too tired to talk, he ate a little food before collapsing from exhaustion. When he woke the next morning he told his mother exactly what had happened the day before, describing all of the evil things his supposed uncle had done.

"Oh, my poor boy!" cried his mother. "That low-down dog, he has abused my son, and my trust – he deserves to die a thousand deaths."

Aladdin replied, "Mother I promise I shall never be any trouble again – give me some breakfast please and I will go to work like a man."

"Alas my son," said his mother, "you ate all that we had last night. Wait until I sell some of my clothes and then we'll eat."

"No mother, why don't we sell this lamp instead?"

The mother took the lamp and tried to give it a quick clean. She had hardly begun rubbing it when a huge, ugly creature appeared – it was another genie. It bowed low and said,

"I am your humble servant. Order and I shall obey!"

Well, Aladdin's mother nearly died of fright. However, Aladdin was getting quite used to this now and promptly ordered the genie to bring them some food. The genie bowed and disappeared, only to reappear immediately with twelve huge, silver platters heaped with the finest food and a pair of solid gold goblets filled with drink. The genie returned to the lamp, leaving the astounded mother speechless.

Over the following days, whenever Aladdin and his mother needed money they sold one of the platters the genie had brought. The merchants of the souk were so impressed with Aladdin's good manners and honest nature that they grew to love him. When Aladdin showed them the fruits he had brought back from the underground garden they were only too happy to explain that they were not glass balls but precious gems – rubies, emeralds, sapphires and diamonds. Aladdin and his mother were now rich beyond their wildest dreams! Even so, they still lived modestly, and made sure they gave plenty of money to the poor.

One morning when Aladdin was walking down the street, the sultan's guards arrived shouting: "Back indoors! Clear the streets! The Sultan's daughter is going to the bathhouse. Anyone who lays eyes upon her will be punished with death!"

Aladdin was consumed with an insatiable curiosity to see what the princess looked like. He quickly ran to the bathhouse, hid behind the door and waited for her. When she arrived and took off her veil Aladdin's heart flipped over in his chest – she was truly beautiful! Her eyes were big and bright, her lips a vibrant red, her face, as flawless as a pearl, was framed by long black hair. Aladdin immediately fell deeply in love.

When he returned home, Aladdin flopped onto the couch and sat there staring into space. When his mother asked what was wrong, Aladdin confessed he was love-struck. "I can't help thinking about the Sultan's daughter. If I don't marry her I'm sure I'll die."

His mother did all she could to discourage him. "Remember," she said, "you are only the son of a poor tailor." But Aladdin would not listen, and faced with such persistence, his mother saw she must help him. Trembling with fear, she went to the sultan and asked whether their children might marry. She took as a gift a golden platter filled with jewels. The sultan imagined such a fabulously expensive gift could only come from some mysterious rich prince, and agreed

that Aladdin and his daughter would be wed within three months.

Aladdin and his mother spent the next few weeks preparing for the wedding. One day while out for a walk, the mother was astonished to see the whole city preparing for a fete. She asked a merchant what was happening.

"How can't you have heard?" he replied. "The princess is getting married today to the son of a vizier."

Alas, it was true. The sultan had been persuaded by an ambitious official to allow his son to marry the sultan's daughter rather than Aladdin.

The news struck Aladdin and his mother like a hammer blow, but Aladdin had an idea. He rubbed the lantern and summoned the genie to ask him for help.

"Genie, when the princess and the vizier's son go to bed, move them. Take the vizier's son to a locked room. Take me to the princess' room and then bring us both back here."

The genie obeyed in a trice. The princess was alarmed to find herself flying through the air on her bed, but Aladdin reassured her.

"Princess, do not fear. Your father promised your hand to me. I will not harm you, but I cannot allow you to stay with that man."

He placed his sabre between them so she could see that he meant her no harm. As the genie carried them through the night air they both drifted off to sleep. In the morning, the genie took Aladdin home before releasing the princess' husband from the locked room and taking him and his bride back to the palace.

The following night the same thing happened. In the morning the sultan, spying his daughter's confused expression, asked what was wrong. She told him of the amazing adventures that she went on each night that were thrilling and frightening in equal measure. The sultan was furious. "A husband should protect his wife – it appears he cannot manage that most sacred duty! I annul this marriage immediately!"

Three months had passed since the sultan had promised Aladdin's mother that their offspring would marry, so Aladdin sent his mother to the palace once more to claim what was pledged. However the vizier was a jealous man, and tried to stop the marriage. He persuaded the sultan to ask Aladdin for an impossible dowry: forty gold dishes filled with precious stones, carried by eighty slaves – forty young girls and forty young boys – each dressed in the finest clothes.

When his mother returned with the news, Aladdin smiled. He summoned the genie and instructed it not only to satisfy the sultan's demands, but surpass them.

Aladdin arrived at the palace on a horse wearing diamond-encrusted reins, followed by one hundred slaves and camels, each carrying a gold dish filled with precious stones. The sultan was speechless and was more than happy to give his daughter's hand in marriage. For her part, the princess had already fallen in love with Aladdin so the ceremony passed with much rejoicing, music and feasting.

The day after the wedding, Aladdin asked the sultan for a site to build a palace. When one was found Aladdin had the genie build them the most fabulous home in the land; with jewelled domes and window-frames studded with precious stones. Aladdin and the princess lived there for many happy years. They also took care of the poor people that lived around, and for this they were much loved and admired.

Meanwhile, in distant Africa, the magician sat in his room brooding on his failure. To cheer himself up, he peered into his crystal ball to look at the dead body of Aladdin. Imagine his surprise when he saw that, far from being dead, Aladdin was rich, married and happy! The magician cursed, realising Aladdin must have discovered the secret of the lamp. Immediately he left for Arabia, all the while plotting his revenge.

The magician arrived at the city with a number of new lamps. He wandered the streets of the souk crying out: "New lamps! New lamps! Who would like to swap their old lamp for a new one?" This strange offer caught the attention of the people in the market and they dashed home to fetch their old lamps to swap. The princess heard the magician too, and remembered her husband kept an old lamp in his room. "How he would love a new lamp instead of that tatty old thing," she thought. She dispatched a servant to take the lamp and exchange it for a new one. The magician had his revenge – and his lamp!

That night the magician rubbed the lamp. The genie appeared, saying: "I am your humble servant. Order and I shall obey!" The magician replied: "While Aladdin is out, take the princess and their palace to my home in Africa." The genie did so. Later, when the sultan realised his daughter's home had disappeared he was horrified! The vizier, still bitter after all these years, said to him, "Your Excellency, didn't I say that that palace must have been the work of a demon?" The sultan flew into a rage: "This is down to that traitor, Aladdin!" he cried. "I want him caught and executed!"

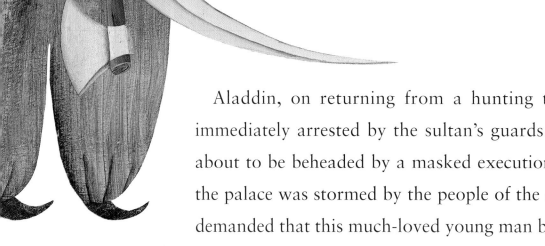

Aladdin, on returning from a hunting trip, was immediately arrested by the sultan's guards. He was about to be beheaded by a masked executioner when the palace was stormed by the people of the city, who demanded that this much-loved young man be spared.

Having escaped death, Aladdin slipped quietly from the city and, filled with despair, wandered through the desert alone for days. Absent-mindedly he rubbed his ring and immediately the genie appeared. "I am the genie of the ring. Your wish is my command," it said.

This genie was not as powerful as the lamp genie, so it could not break the magician's spell. Aladdin realised cunning would also be needed to reverse the magician's magic. "Take me to the princess," commanded Aladdin, "and bring a powerful poison."

In a wink Aladdin found himself beside his wife. She told him that each evening the magician came to her room and tried to persuade her to marry him. Aladdin took the poison from his pocket and gave it to her. "When he comes to your room this evening," said Aladdin, "pour this into his cup. It is our only hope of escape."

The princess carried out the plan to the letter. When the magician took a swig of his wine he fell to the floor in agony. Desperately he tried to pull the lamp from his robes to seek the genie's help. But Aladdin, who had been hiding behind the curtains, wrestled it from the magician's hands.

"You son of a dog!" cried the magician. "How I would love to strangle the very life from you with…" And he breathed no more.

Aladdin did not waste a second. He commanded the genie to take them and the palace back home. The sultan's heart nearly burst with delight when he saw them arrive. After checking that his daughter was unharmed, he realised that he had misjudged Aladdin.

"You are a good man, true and brave," he said to Aladdin. "You have risked much for my precious daughter. When I am gone my kingdom shall be yours."

The king died a few years later. Aladdin became sultan and his rule was just and fair. And the lamp? The lamp became a distant memory.

THE **POLAR BEAR SON**

In the frozen land near the North Pole, where all there is to see is snow and ice, there was a small village. In this village lived an old lady who had neither a husband nor any children. She did not go hungry though, for the people of the village would give her food after they had been hunting. Some days it would be whale or seal meat, other days blubber, and occasionally some bear.

One day, when the men of the village were out hunting they discovered a frozen bear. To their great surprise, they found a small cub inside it. The men thought the cub was dead too, and took it back to the village for the old woman.

"Would you like to have this bear cub?" they asked her.

The old lady accepted, as a bear cub would keep her fed for many a day. She took the cub into her house to thaw it ready for cooking. But as the bear got warmer the old woman noticed it moving – the bear wasn't dead at all! Gently the old woman picked it up and sat it next to the fire. She then melted down some blubber for the bear to drink. After drinking, the bear sniffed at the old woman and fell asleep.

The old woman was delighted to have a companion. She called him Little Bear and fed him seal meat and gave him melted blubber to drink. The old woman talked to him as if he were her son, rather than a pet.

As the bear got older, the children of the village would come to play with him, shouting through the old woman's window:

"Little Bear, Little Bear, come out to play."

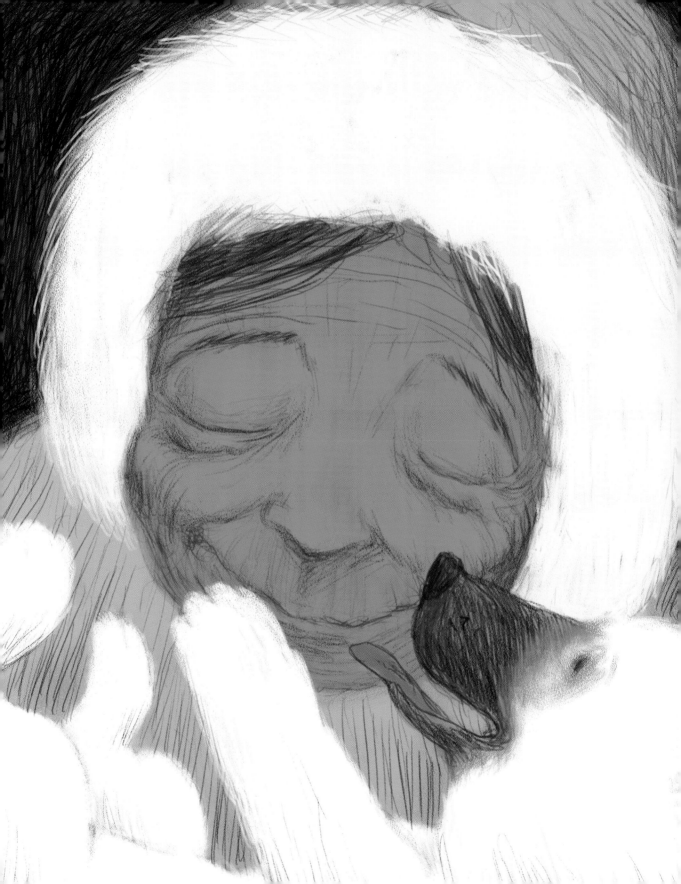

The bear would sniff at the old woman and go out through the window. Little Bear and the children would play together and the bear would take care to make sure he kept his claws sheathed so as not to hurt them. But as the bear got older and bigger he became too strong for the children. He would break their toy harpoons and when he pushed them, the children would get hurt and cry.

Now that he was too big to play with the children, Little Bear would wrestle with the hunters for exercise and grew bigger and stronger because of it. Soon Little Bear was not so little any more. In fact he was too big and strong for even the men of the village to play with. They said to one another:

"We should take the bear with us when we go hunting. He would help us to find seals."

So one day, at dawn, the men came to the old woman's window and said:

"Little Bear, Little Bear, come out with us and help us hunt."

The bear sniffed at the old woman as he always did and climbed out through the window to help the men. On the way the men explained to Little Bear that he had to stay downwind of the seals otherwise they might smell him and swim off.

With Little Bear's help the hunt was a great success. The bear's sharp sense of smell could pick out a seal from many kilometres away. Little Bear would then lie by the hole in the ice which the seals used to breathe through. He would stay by the hole for many hours, without moving a muscle, until a seal poked its nose out of the freezing water. Then, quick as a flash, the bear would swipe with one of his mighty paws and kill the seal.

By the end of the day, Little Bear and the hunters had gathered enough meat for the village. When they returned, Little Bear proudly brought his share to the old woman.

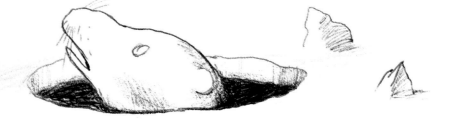

One evening after the hunt the men called in to see the old woman.

"Do not worry old woman, but Little Bear has been hurt. He was attacked by hunters from the north who did not realise who he was. He needs to have a collar so people can recognise him."

That night the old woman plaited thick strands of hair together and made Little Bear a beautiful collar to wear.

"My dear Little Bear," said the old woman. "I never wanted to put a collar on you, for you are like a son to me, not some kind of pet. But you are in danger now, so you must wear this collar whenever you hunt. That way other people will not think you are a wild bear, but will know that you are my son. Whenever you see people from other villages, do not attack them unless you are in danger."

Now everyone could spot Little Bear, even the hunters from different villages. Little Bear grew bigger and stronger and was the best hunter in all the villages in that cold and frosty land. He always caught a seal, no matter what the weather or time of year.

The hunters from other villages knew what a good hunter Little Bear was and were jealous of him. One of them even said:

"If I get the chance I will kill him!"

The people of that village were outraged.

"How can you say that?" they asked. "He catches food for an old woman. She loves him like a son. Where would she get food from if you were to kill her bear?"

One day the bear was out hunting and there was a terrible storm. He did not return until late that evening. He climbed through the window and sniffed at the old woman as usual but something wasn't quite right. The old woman looked outside and there was the body of a man. She hurried to the nearest house.

"Are you all safe?" cried the woman.

"Yes," her neighbours replied. "Why do you ask?"

"Little Bear has come home with a body and I don't know who it might be," replied the old woman.

In the morning the villagers inspected the body. It was a man from one of the villages in the north. Soon the dead man's friends arrived. They told the old woman how the man had attacked Little Bear and how they had to persuade Little Bear to defend himself.

So the bear had been attacked by a man and had killed him. The old woman was very sad. She now worried when Little Bear went out to hunt with the men that it would happen again.

One day she called the bear to her and said:

"Little Bear, this place is no longer safe for you. Sooner or later someone else will be jealous of how well you hunt and they will attack you. If they do not kill you someone else will try again later on, for that is the way with men. You have your own kind living not far away from here. You should go and join them for you will be safer with them."

Little Bear was sad to hear this for he loved the old woman. He nuzzled up close and sniffed at her. The old woman took off Little Bear's collar so no one would recognise him. She hugged the bear for one last time and kissed him on the nose. At the same time she secretly rubbed some soot on the polar bear's belly so she alone would be able to spot him if their paths ever crossed again.

The bear sniffed at the old woman one more time, then climbed out through the window and left. The old woman cried, for she had loved the bear like a son. The rest of the village mourned his leaving, too, for Little Bear was a great hunter and a brave companion.

As for Little Bear, no one knows exactly what became of him, but hunters from the north told stories of an enormous bear with a black spot on his belly that was better at catching seals than any hunter alive.

KEKEDIOUROU AND THE WITCH

In a country in West Africa there was a pregnant woman. One day she heard from her belly a little voice shouting, "Mother give birth to me!"

The poor woman was stunned. She thought for a moment before replying, "Can't a baby who can speak by himself not be born by himself, too?"

Without further ado the baby brought himself into the world right there and then, with no help from a single living person.

The child looked at his mother and said, "Mother, wash me."

The woman replied, "Surely a child who can be born by himself is capable of washing himself?"

The child washed, and then asked his mother for a name. Again his mother suggested he should give himself one. He chose "Kekediourou", which means "He who is not afraid of witches". Then Kekediourou asked his mother who his father was. She replied, "He is dead, but you do have two brothers. They are on their way to the village of wizards."

"In which case," said the child, raising himself, "I will go and protect them from the wizards." And taking a sickle and fishing net, he set off on the road to find his brothers.

A fearsome queen ruled the village of the wizards. She was a powerful witch, whose cruelty caused misery in the surrounding area. Armed with little more than their courage, the two brothers had decided to rid themselves of this evil. However, a witch is not an easy foe to overcome…

The very road to the village itself was bewitched. Hungry dogs and bulls waited there, ready to devour anyone who passed. The two brothers were ignorant of such magic and were about to be leapt upon when Kekediourou arrived to save them. "My brothers, do not fear!" he cried. He threw down a huge bundle of grass, which he had cut with the sickle for the bulls. For the dogs he had some fish which he had caught in his net. The two brothers were grateful for his help, but refused to allow Kekediourou to come with them.

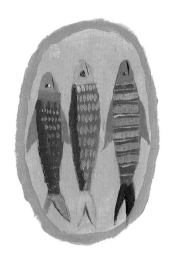

"You cannot be our brother," they said. "Our mother had not given birth when we left home."

And every time Kekediourou tried to follow them, they chased him off with harsh blows and harsher words. However, Kekediourou was not to be thwarted. Using his magical powers, he turned himself into a hat and appeared on the path in front of his brothers. Spying the hat, the oldest brother said, "Aha, a hat! That would be perfect for shading my head from the sun." And he popped it on his head. To his surprise, the hat started to speak. "My brother, it's not a hat – it's me, Kekediourou!" At that, the brother whipped off his hat and threw it away.

Kekediourou then turned himself into a beautiful ring and again appeared on the road in front of his brothers. The other brother spotted the ring lying there and picked it up. Kekediourou immediately piped up, "My brothers, it is me Kekediourou! You will truly regret it if you don't take me with you. Remember it was me who saved you from the dogs and bulls." The brothers looked at each other for a moment. "Kekediourou, as you are so insistent on joining us, you must really be our brother. You are welcome to come along."

The three brothers arrived at the village of the wizards as the sun was setting and demanded to see the queen. They were shown in immediately. The queen was a terrifying sight. She was extremely tall with a necklace of crocodile teeth around her neck, and long hooked fingers like an eagle's claws. A terrible smell, like death itself, hung around her, attracting a great cloud of constantly buzzing flies.

The witch decided she would devour them that night, but disguising her intentions, she sent them to a room for something to eat. The brothers were given three big bowls filled with couscous. The couscous in the first bowl was mixed with pieces of beef; in the second bowl it was mixed with dog meat; and in the third it was mixed with human flesh. Fortunately Kekediourou realised something was wrong. He ran his fingers through the couscous and spotted that two of the bowls were bad. "Eat only from the first bowl," Kekediourou said, "the other two are filled with the

witch's evil magic." And Kekediourou knew he must stay awake that night to watch out for danger.

Meanwhile the queen was setting a large pot of water to boil, to cook the brothers. At midnight, when she was sure the brothers would be asleep, she went to their room, but Kekediourou shouted out, "You needn't try to come in yet, I'm not asleep."

"And why are you not asleep?" asked the queen.

"Because you did not give me what my father gives me to eat every evening," replied Kekediourou.

"And what does your father give you every evening?" asked the queen, furious that her plans were being ruined.

"He fed me the stars," replied Kekediourou.

"Then you shall have stars," said the queen, "for nothing is impossible for me."

And the witch spent the entire night trying to collect stars, but dawn came before she could catch them.

Before night had fallen the next day, Kekediourou asked a favour of the queen: "Perhaps if you let your three daughters stay in our room tonight we might be able to get to sleep." The queen agreed, for if the magical Kekediourou stayed awake again then she would not be able to kill the brothers.

When the three girls were asleep, Kekediourou cut off their long hair and made wigs for his brothers and himself. Then he pretended to sleep.

Around midnight the witch queen approached the room, with a big hook in her hand. She entered the room quietly and quickly cut the throats of the sleepers with short hair. It was, of course, her own daughters that she had slain. In the meantime, the three brothers had fled back to their village.

The next morning a maidservant told the witch queen the terrible news. The queen dashed to the room and saw the bodies of her daughters. The queen was thrown into such a rage that there was no room left inside her for grief. "This is all because of Kekediourou!" she cried. "I shall wreak my vengeance on him and his village!"

The queen set off immediately and when she reached the outskirts of Kekediourou's village, she changed herself into a glorious jujube tree, all heavy with fruit and rich foliage. As the queen had planned, all of the children from the village were soon clambering all over the tree's branches like a great flock of birds. "Get down!" cried Kekediourou. "It's not a real tree, it's a trap!" But the children ignored him; they were having too much fun. Suddenly the branches of the tree linked up like the bars of a cage and the children were trapped! The tree pulled itself from the ground and set off for the village of the wizards – with Kekediourou in hot pursuit.

When the tree reached the village it returned to its human form. The queen herded the children into a small room and, using an evil spell, walled them in. Happy with her day's work the queen went to rest. Kekediourou saw everything. He couldn't break the spell, but he could use his cunning. "So," he thought, "if there's no door to the room, the children will have to come out another way – under the ground."

Casting a quick spell, Kekediourou turned the children into a colony of ants. Then, using the language of insects, he shouted to them, "Do not be afraid, it is me, Kekediourou. Now, dig a tunnel under the wall and come straight to me."

The children did as Kekediourou said, and one by

one they popped out into the fresh air on the other side of the wall. Kekediourou then turned himself into an ant, too, and led them in procession out of the village. But danger! The queen was walking through the village for her yearly bath. Clump, clump, went her feet and she nearly crushed the line of the ants. She even looked down and watched them scurry away – never realising that they were really the children and Kekediourou.

When they were out of danger, Kekediourou turned the children and himself back into humans. On their return home, the whole village was overjoyed to see them and greeted Kekediourou like a returning king.

When the queen realised what had happened, she flew into a violent rage. She cast a spell and turned herself into a beautiful young lady, dressed in the finest clothes, and went to Kekediourou's village. As soon as she arrived all the young men fell in love with her. "Do not even think about it," she said. "I only have eyes for Moussa and I will marry him." Moussa was Kekediourou's oldest brother.

"Open your eyes, Moussa!" cried Kekediourou. "That's no lady, that's the witch queen!" But Moussa was not listening. He felt flattered to be chosen by such a beautiful lady and married her that evening.

Around midnight the bride rose from her bed. She spat into her hands and rubbed them together, reciting a spell. Looking at her sleeping husband, she said: "May your eyes jump into my hands." No sooner had her words left her lips than Moussa's eyes were in her hands. The queen then left the room and fled back to her village.

The next morning, Moussa discovered that he was blind. "Kekediourou," he called, "I beg you, find my eyes. Without them I am lost."

Kekediourou was outraged by the queen's trick. However, he had a plan. He changed himself to look like one of the queen's nieces and went to her village.

"My dear aunt," said Kekediourou to the queen, "I hear that a boy by the name of Kekediourou has been causing you a great deal of trouble."

"That is quite true, my niece," replied the queen. "But I have gained my vengeance. I have stolen the beautiful eyes of his brother, Moussa." The queen couldn't help but laugh at her cruelty.

"Does that mean he will never be able to see again?" asked Kekediourou.

"Indeed it does, unless I wish otherwise," replied the queen. "There is one powder which can reverse the spell, and I keep that in a chest with my clothes and jewels. All I would have to do is rub his face with the powder and he would be able to see – but I don't plan on doing that!"

Imagine Kekediourou's delight at hearing that bit of news! As soon as the queen was gone, Kekediourou stole into her room, took the powder from the chest, and sped back to his village. He ran straight to his sightless brother and rubbed the powder over Moussa's face. His sight was restored as the queen had said it would be. "Praise be!" cried Moussa. "Thank you my brother, thank you!"

The next day the queen realised she had been tricked yet again. This time she turned herself into a beautiful horse and trotted to Kekediourou's village. Kekediourou spotted the witch's deception, grabbed the horse by the mane and leapt upon its back.

"I recognise you, you old witch," said Kekediourou. "We will only be free of your evil when you are dead." Digging his heels into her sides, Kekediourou forced the horse into a hard gallop through bush and forest, and over the distant mountains. Caught in her own trap, the witch was forced to gallop all day. Eventually, she collapsed, exhausted to the point of death. The queen realised she was defeated. "Curse you, Kekediourou," she gasped. "Your magic is stronger than mine." And with that, she died.

That is how Kekediourou delivered his people from the most terrible witch the country had ever known.

THE DRAGON'S PEARL

In China, many years ago, a boy lived with his mother by the banks of a great river. The mother was very ill, so it was up the boy to find work. He used to go out and gather the thick grass which grew by the river and exchange it for a little food with the people of the nearby village.

One year it was very hot and the rains rarely fell, so all the grass began to dry out and die. Fortunately for the boy, he found a patch of grass that was still thick and fresh, even though all the grass around it was dead. As he began to gather some into his arms, he spotted a small, bright ball on the ground. He picked it up with the grass and hurried home.

"This looks like a dragon's pearl," thought the boy. "I've seen a dragon carrying one of these in his mouth in the paintings on the temple walls." In those times dragons were not feared, on the contrary they were respected, for they had the power to make the rains come which was good for the crops.

Thrilled with his discovery, the boy raced home. He showed his mother the pearl and said: "Mother, look what I found while I was out harvesting the grass. Hide it somewhere safe and I'll go off to sell it tomorrow."

As the rice jar was nearly empty his mother put the pearl in that.

The next day when the mother went to fetch the pearl from the jar she had a huge surprise – the jar was full to the brim with rice!

"How can this be?" she cried, showing her son.

"It's the dragon's pearl," said the boy. "It had made all the grass grow where I had found it. Now it has made the rice multiply because you put it in the rice jar. That must be the way with dragons' pearls."

That night the mother put the pearl inside her purse. When they awoke the next morning it was bursting with gold coins.

Now, thanks to the dragon's pearl the mother and her son wanted for nothing. If they needed food the pearl provided it; if they needed money, the same. Being good people they made sure that their neighbours benefited from their fortune. The village did not go hungry that year, even though the lack of

rain ruined the harvest. However the mother, unable to keep a secret, told the story of the pearl.

Some people in the village were jealous of the mother's good fortune, for there are those who cannot abide seeing others more happy than themselves.

"We should have that pearl," they said.

And one evening they banded together, armed themselves with clubs, and went to the house of the mother and her son.

"Give us the dragon's pearl!" they cried.

They pushed the mother aside and began to ransack the house.

This made the boy so angry that he swallowed the pearl, rather than hand it over. Immediately, he began to burn up inside. He quickly drank some water to try to ease the pain. "More, more," cried the boy. "It burns, it burns!" His mother handed him a big pitcher of water, which he drank in one gulp. But the boy was still thirsty. He dashed to the riverbank and stuck his head in the river and drank and drank. All of the

people of the village came to see what was going on. They couldn't quite believe their eyes.

As the boy took huge gulps from the river, the sky suddenly started to turn black as huge clouds rolled in from all sides. The sky lit up as lightning forked from cloud to cloud. Big, heavy drops of rain began to fall to the ground. The villagers fell to their knees in thanks.

With all of their faces to the sky, the villagers did not notice what was happening to the boy. Two long horns had sprouted from his head and his body was stretching longer and longer. Not only that, he was now covered in scales, like a fish. He sprouted claws at the ends of his hands and grew fearsome teeth in his long face. With a beat of his new wings the boy flew into the air. He had turned into a dragon!

His mother cried out for the boy to come back, but there was nothing that could be done. The pearl had changed the boy and there was no amount of love in the world that could change him back. The boy wept in sorrow and his tears fell to the ground and filled the river below.

As a way of saying goodbye, the dragon slowly twirled around in the sky twenty-four times and each time he shed a tear. Each of these tears formed a small lake when they fell to the ground and these lakes still exist to this day.

After twirling in the sky, the dragon then dived into the lake and was never seen again.

FALLING STAR

One summer night, two Cheyenne girls were lying outside their tepee. They stared up at the night sky imagining patterns which the stars made and looking for their favourite stars.

"Look at that one," said the first girl, "that's the star I like."

"I prefer that one," said the second girl.

The girls stared up at the sky for a while longer. The first girl pointed to a brilliantly bright star and said:

"No, that's the one for me. It's the brightest star of all. I'd like to marry that star."

The next morning the two girls went to collect some firewood. When they reached the forest they spotted a porcupine climbing a tall tree.

"I'll climb up and catch it," said the first girl.

She was up the tree like a flash, but when she got close the porcupine climbed a little bit higher.

"Come down," shouted the second girl, "the tree is growing taller!"

It was true; the tree was definitely growing before her very eyes.

"No!" replied the first girl, following the porcupine up the tree.

The second girl knew it was too dangerous, so she rushed back to the camp for help. However by the time she had come back to the tree with her people, the first girl had disappeared from sight!

The tree continued to grow. Eventually the first girl reached another world entirely – the place the Cheyenne call the World of In-high. The tree stopped growing and the girl stepped off the branch and on to a cloud. There, waiting for her, was a man. He smiled at her, but the girl burst into tears.

"Why are you crying?" he asked. "Just last night I heard you say you wanted to marry me. I am the brightest star."

The girl was overjoyed to meet the brightest star, and her dream came true as they married immediately. The Cheyenne girl quickly grew used to the World of In-High. The brightest star explained to the girl that she could dig up any wild vegetable she liked with the other star-women, but she should never pull up the

great white turnips with the large green leaves. To harvest these would be against the will of the sky god.

Every day the girl went to pick the wild vegetables and every day she wondered why she wasn't allowed to pull up the big white turnips. As each day passed her curiosity grew stronger, and eventually she decided to pull up one of the forbidden turnips. She tugged at the green leaves, but the turnip wouldn't move. She pulled with all her might and slowly, slowly the turnip came out of the ground. The girl was exhausted when she finished. She looked into the hole that the turnip had come out of and saw far below her the camp where she used to live.

Everything looked tiny – the teepees and villagers were just small specks on the ground. Seeing them made her feel terribly homesick; but she was so high up and they were so far away, how would she get back down? Then she noticed that there was some long, thick grass growing near the hole. "If I could twist the grass together," thought the girl, "I could make a rope and climb down to my old home." No sooner had she thought of the idea than she was twisting the grass together to make a rope. Each day she worked on the rope and each day it got a little longer.

At long last she was finished. She tied one end of the rope to a large log to act as an anchor and threw the other end out of the hole. To her delight the end of the rope seemed to reach the ground.

The girl slid through the hole and slowly began to slide down the rope. It took a long time to descend, for the rope was so long. Finally she reached the end of the rope, but disaster struck – the rope wasn't long enough. She was left dangling in the air crying out for

help; but her words were carried away on the wind and no one heard to come to her aid. Eventually, she could hold on no more and fell to her death on the ground. The girl was pregnant, but her unborn son did not die because he was made of star stone and was therefore unbreakable.

A skylark saw what had happened. She swooped down and picked up the baby and took it back to her nest. She called the baby Falling Star and he grew up with the skylark's family. As they grew bigger and stronger, so did Falling Star. When they learnt to fly, Falling Star learnt to run; and the faster they flew, the quicker Falling Star ran.

One day Mother Skylark said to Falling Star:

"It is time for you to join your own people. The cold weather is approaching and my family and I need to fly south."

"Mother Skylark," replied Falling Star, "why are you trying to drive me away? I want to come with you all, too."

"No, my son," said Mother Skylark, "you must return home now."

"I will go then," said Falling Star, "if Father Skylark makes me a bow and arrows."

Father Skylark made a bow for Falling Star and then he made four arrows, using his own feathers for the flights. He then pointed Falling Star in the direction of his people who were living further downstream by the banks of the river.

Falling Star set off on the long journey to his people. Eventually he reached their camp and went into an old woman's tepee.

"Grandmother," he said, "I would like a drink of water."

"My young boy," she replied, "only the fastest

young men can collect water. There is a monster in the river who eats up anyone who gets too close."

"Grandmother, if you give me your ladle of buffalo horn and your buffalo hide pouch, I will collect the water."

"Oh my grandson, take care. The monster has already killed many young men, I don't want you to die too," said the grandmother, handing him the ladle and pouch.

The moment Falling Star drew his first ladle of water, a great monster raised its head above the river. It had an enormous mouth and with one bite he

swallowed the ladle, the pouch and Falling Star. Inside the creature's stomach, Falling Star could see all the other people the monster had swallowed. Taking a piece of star stone that Falling Star always carried with him, he cut a hole in the monster's side so all the people could escape. Falling Star took the pouch and the ladle and brought some fresh water home for the old woman.

She was amazed to see him alive. "Who *are* you?" she asked.

"I am Falling Star, I have come from the sky. I have killed the monster in the river and freed all the people."

The old woman went to the village to tell all the good news that the monster was dead.

Falling Star then asked the old woman if there were any other camps nearby.

"Yes," she replied, "there is another camp further down the river."

Falling Star took his bow and arrows and left the camp. After travelling for a number of days he reached the other village. Again he entered the tepee of an old woman, who was sitting next to her fire.

"Grandmother, I am hungry," he said.

"My boy, my boy, we have nothing to eat. Every time our men go to hunt, a gigantic white crow warns the buffalo of the hunter's approach and they flee."

"How sad," said Falling Star. "I will help. Find me an old buffalo robe and tell your chief to send me the two fastest runners in the camp."

When the old woman returned with the skin and the runners, Falling Star explained his plan. "I will wait for the buffalo," he said. "When the

herd runs, I will run with them as you chase us," he said, pointing to the runners. "You will pretend to shoot me with your arrows and I will fall down as if dead. You will then make as if to cut open my stomach, then you will abandon my body to the sun."

Falling Star dressed as a buffalo and waited for the herd. When the buffalo arrived, the two hunters started to stalk the animals. Immediately, the white crow appeared shouting:

"They're coming, the hunters are coming! Run!"

The herd of buffalo took flight with Falling Star amongst them. The two hunters followed their part of their plan and pretended to shoot and leave Falling Star. Many were attracted to the body, including wolves, coyotes and the white crow. It flew backwards and forwards over it, calling out "Is that Falling Star? Is that Falling Star?"

Each time the crow flew past calling "Is that Falling Star?" he flew a little bit closer to the body. Soon he was flying so close that Falling Star could jump up and grab the crow's legs. Seeing this, all the other animals fled.

Falling Star took the crow to the old woman and asked her to fetch the chief of the camp. The chief was overjoyed and said:

"I shall take the crow to my house and tie him to the smoke hole until he is dead."

And from that day the good Cheyenne people had plenty of buffalo to eat.

As a token of thanks, the Cheyenne gave Falling Star a home of his own. Waiting inside was a pretty young girl. They got married and spent the rest of their lives living with the Cheyenne of the north.

However Falling Star never forgot where he came from – the world of the sky people. Every evening he would leave the camp and spend a few minutes scanning the sky, looking for his father, the brightest star of all.

THE RUBY PRINCE

O nce upon a time in a village in India a brahmin, which is a kind of holy man, used to walk to the temple every day to pray to the gods.

One day while he walked along the road, he spotted something shining amongst the stones on the ground. He bent down and saw that it was a bright red stone. It looked so pretty that the brahmin put it in his pocket. Further down the road he passed a corn-seller. The smell of the corn cooking on the grill reminded the brahmin that he had not eaten all day. However, he did not have a single rupee about his person, so he offered the stone to the corn-seller in exchange for some food. Fortunately the corn-seller was honest.

"Are you mad?" he cried. "That is a ruby and it's worth more than my entire shop. You'd better take that to the palace to show the king."

The brahmin gave the stone a rub to clean the dust off. It gleamed a bright blood red and glowed as if it had been lit by a thousand fires. It was undoubtedly a beautiful stone. When he showed it to the king, the ruler was overjoyed and insisted on paying the brahmin a small fortune for it.

The king then called his wife, the queen. "Look at this exquisite ruby. There is nothing to match it in the whole world. I entrust it to you. Take care of it and it will always bring us happiness." The queen took the stone and carefully placed it in a solid trunk with double locks.

One morning, twelve years later, the king decided that he wanted to check on the ruby, to make sure it was still safe after all these years. However, when the queen opened the trunk the ruby was gone and in its place was

a handsome boy. "Who are you?" demanded the king. "And what have you done with my ruby?"

"Your ruby no longer exists," said the boy. "I have taken its place. I am the Ruby Prince. I cannot tell you how this happened, for it is not for you to know."

The king was silent for a moment and then exploded into a furious rage. "My ruby is stolen and replaced by a so-called prince and you offer no explanation! Such insolence! Leave my palace immediately!"

Despite his rage, the king was a decent enough man to ensure the boy was given a horse and sword before he left.

The Ruby Prince mounted his steed and rode for the rest of the day. Eventually he came to the gates of a city, where there was an old woman in tears. "Why the tears, old lady?" he asked.

"My son is to die today," she replied. "A gigantic flesh-eating demon terrorises our homes. Every day he demands a young boy to eat or he will destroy the city. It has been decreed that my son must give up his life tonight, and it breaks my heart to lose him."

"Do not fear, old lady," replied the Ruby Prince. "I will kill the monster and free the city from this curse. Point out this demon to me."

"It will be no use," said the old lady. "He will kill you today instead and then my son tomorrow."

"You may not believe me," said the prince, "but I will kill the demon."

Just as night was about to fall, the prince arrived at the spot where the demon normally appeared. The prince tied his horse out of the way and then settled down on the ground beneath a blanket and fell asleep. Before too long, a huge roar split the night air and the

demon approached. The prince had a plan, though, and stayed exactly where he was, hidden under his blanket.

The demon could not see anyone and believed that the city had not left him his daily meal of human flesh. He was furious and let out a mighty howl that shook the very tops of the trees. At that moment, the prince leapt from his hiding place and sliced off the demon's head with one powerful swipe of his sword.

When the Ruby Prince returned to the city, carrying the monster's head aloft, he was greeted like a hero. The news of his great deed soon reached the ears of the king. He requested that the Ruby Prince come to the palace to be rewarded for his courage. Imagine the

king's surprise when he discovered that the warrior who had slain the monster was the same boy who had popped out of his trunk! As a gesture of his gratitude, he gave the Ruby Prince his daughter's hand in marriage. Everyone in the kingdom was thrilled with the union.

The young princess was completely captivated by the Ruby Prince's beauty and generous nature. She loved him completely, yet one thing worried her. She,

like everyone else, knew nothing about him. No one knew where he came from or who his family were. The prince was shrouded in mystery. One evening the princess said to him: "I love you, but I know almost nothing about you. Please tell me who you are and where you come from." The prince replied, "My dearest love, I will tell you anything you ask of me but please do not ask me that, for that is the one thing I cannot tell you."

The princess did not press the issue, but each day that passed made her more curious. Eventually she asked the prince again, but he answered her sharply: "Do not seek to know what you will regret when you discover it!"

As the days passed the princess became tormented by the need to know the prince's secret. One day while walking together in their garden, she asked again. "If you love me," said the princess, "entrust me with your secret." The prince refused. "You know I cannot do that," he replied. "I, I beg you tell me," she cried, her eyes filled with tears. The couple had reached the river that flowed past the bottom of their garden. The prince walked towards it.

He stared at the water with a sad look upon his face and then waded into the river. "In which case, know that I am the son of the king of snakes and that...." Before he could finish, his head disappeared beneath the water. A serpent with a ruby on top of its head rose out of the river, stared at the princess, then dived back.

Desperately, the princess ran up and down the bank calling the prince's name.

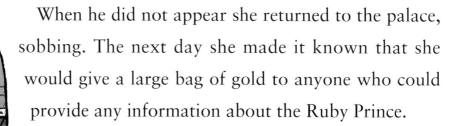

When he did not appear she returned to the palace, sobbing. The next day she made it known that she would give a large bag of gold to anyone who could provide any information about the Ruby Prince.

Long months passed without any news of her love. The princess spent her days weeping with regret for her insatiable curiosity which had lost her her beloved husband. She became thinner and paler with each passing day.

Then one day a dancer from the palace came to the princess. "Last night," she said, "I was asleep beneath a tree when I was awoken by a strange light, quite unlike the sun or moon's. Then, from out of a snake hole, came some servants who swept the ground and sprinkled water on it before laying down a sumptuous rug. Music sounded and from the hole came a procession of young men wearing glittering jewels. They were followed by a man who seemed to be their king as he had a crown on his head. The men danced before the king and there was one man with a bright red stone on his head. He danced too, but looked pale and weak. That is all I have to tell you."

The following night, the princess went with the dancer to the tree to see if the same thing would happen again. True enough after a long wait the strange light shone and the servants appeared, followed by the procession of dancers and musicians.

The princess' heart was fit to break when she saw her husband, the Ruby Prince, so pale and frail, dancing for the king.

When everyone had danced, the strange light disappeared and the people vanished. The princess returned to the palace full of sorrow. Each night she returned to the same spot to catch a glimpse of her husband as he danced. Her heart remained heavy, as she had no idea how to get the Ruby Prince to return to her.

Then one day the dancer came to the princess with an idea. "Only men seem to dance for the king," she said. "What would happen if I were to dance for him? He might be so happy that who knows what he would give me as a reward."

"No," replied the princess. "I will dance for him, but you must teach me your art."

The dancer taught the princess everything she knew and soon there was no finer or more elegant a dancer than the princess.

When she was ready, the princess dressed herself in fine silks and veils embedded with so many diamonds she shone like a star. With beating heart she waited by the tree. The light shone, the servants and then the musicians and the king appeared and the dancing started. The ruby prince seemed even paler and sadder

than before, and when he danced he was so weak he could hardly move.

Then the princess walked onto the rug and danced for the king. When she finished the king said, "Oh mysterious dancer, never before have I seen such graceful dancing. Tell me your wish and I shall grant it!

The princess tore off her veil. "Give me back my love, the Ruby Prince!" she cried.

The king glared at her and said: "I should kill you for making such a demand, but as I made a promise, take him and he must remain with you for ever!"

The princess took the Ruby Prince by the hand and fled.

The princess and the Ruby Prince spent many years together in blissful happiness. Never again did the princess mention her husband's secret, nor did she ask him to explain the wondrous scenes she had witnessed.

POPOC AND IXTLA

A long time ago Mexico was ruled by the Aztec emperor Moctezuma. He was treated like a god by the Aztec people and was feared and admired by all. The emperor and his family lived a life of complete luxury and the walls of their palace shimmered with gold.

Moctezuma had a number of daughters and like all Aztec girls they were brought up to be proud, but courteous. They also went to the Calmecac, the temple school, as the Aztecs prized a good education. One of the daughters was called Iztaccihuatkl, or Ixtla for short. She was not only courageous and intelligent, but she was very beautiful too.

One day, while walking through the floating gardens of the city, Ixtla stopped to watch

a group of boys. They were trying to get a statuette from the top of a greasy pole. They all failed to get the statue, apart from one boy, called Popocatepetl – or Popoc for short. Instead of trying to climb the pole, he rocked it back and forth until the statue fell to the ground at Ixtla's feet. Popoc and Ixtla stared at each other. Ixtla felt her heart beating faster than a hummingbird's. "He is no more than a trainee warrior," thought Ixtla, "so how does he have the nerve to stare at the emperor's daughter?" For his part, Popoc had fallen madly in love.

That evening Popoc climbed the wall of the palace and went to the aviary, which was where Ixtla kept her pet birds. He gave a love-letter to a beautiful quetzal bird to deliver to her window. Ixtla's reply was swift:

"Your boldness shows a keen heart, but you must be brave in deed as well as with words to win my hand."

From that moment, Popoc had only one aim, to be the greatest warrior in the land.

For many moons, Popoc learnt how to handle a sharp sword and dreamt of victory in glorious battles. "When will I get my chance to impress the emperor?" he wondered.

He did not have long to wait. Popoc was part of the army sent to fight a nearby tribe. In those times the Aztecs did not kill their enemies in battle, but captured them instead to sacrifice later to their god Huitzilopochtli. Popoc fought well that day and captured eight prisoners – a great achievement.

As he hoped, the emperor recognised Popoc's bravery and made him a "war jaguar" – a soldier of high rank. He now wore a jaguar skin and carried a shield decorated with green and turquoise feathers. Popoc decided to ask the emperor for Ixtla's hand in marriage.

The emperor was more than happy to have such a warrior marry his daughter. The wedding ceremony was very impressive. Ixtla looked resplendent in a gold dress with bracelets made of red feathers on her arms and legs. Popoc wore a garment made of shimmering hummingbird feathers. Their tunics were tied together as tradition demanded, and they drank chocolate together out of golden cups. They were now married.

Their joy was short-lived, however. A few days after their wedding, an enemy tribe invaded the country and laid waste to several villages. They were now threatening the capital city, Tenochtitlan, itself. The king assembled all his warriors.

Popoc answered his emperor's call immediately. Ixtla bade him goodbye with a heavy heart. "My love," she said, "I have a terrible feeling about this – I fear for your life."

Ixtla prayed to the Tlazolteotl, the goddess of love. "I cannot offer anything to Huitzilopochtli," said Ixtla, "as he only accepts the blood of warriors. But you, my goddess, please accept my offering and protect the one I love."

The battle was terrible. The crush of bodies and the piercing cries were terrifying to behold. Popoc, who fought at the very front, saved many Aztec lives with his courage and skill. Thanks to him, they won the battle that day.

The defeated army looked for revenge. Some of them disguised themselves as Aztec warriors and went to Tenochtitlan. There they told everyone that Popoc had been killed in the fighting.

The rumour sped round the city that night. The next morning Ixtla was woken by the sound of people wailing and crying outside, wracked with grief for the loss of the bravest warrior of all.

The princess went immediately to the temple and asked all the attendants to leave so that she might be alone with the gods. She then climbed the thousand steps to the top of the temple and threw herself off without a cry.

The next morning the Aztec army returned to the city. Popoc was greeted as a hero. The welcome was more special because it was as if he had returned from the dead. However, when he heard of Ixtla's suicide he felt a pain greater than any he had felt in battle. Quietly he removed his fine warrior robes and went to find his love's body. Then, taking her in his arms, he walked out into the night.

Popoc did not return to the city that night. The next morning the people of Tenochtitlan looked out and saw in the distance two new mountains. One was the shape of a woman lying down; the other was the shape of a kneeling man.

As the people stared at this remarkable sight, a young girl piped up from the middle of the crowd: "Look, one of the mountains is spitting fire!"

Since then, Popocatepetl, whose name means "mountain of fire", occasionally shows his sadness by spouting flames into the air. Over time Iztaccihuatkl, which means "the beautiful dead", has been gently covered with a blanket of ash from the other mountain which looks like everlasting snow.

Even today, the people of Tenochtitlan, now known as Mexico City, still look fondly upon the two mountains; the dead princess guarded forever by her warrior husband.

BABA YAGA

Once long ago in a dark forest far away there lived a young girl called Vassilissa, with her father. Vassilissa's mother had died so her father had married again. Unfortunately while Vassilissa's mother had been kind and beautiful, her stepmother was cruel and spiteful. She treated Vassilissa like a servant: "Do this, do that!" she would shout. She would beat Vassilissa for the slightest reason.

One day, when the father had gone to the city, the stepmother decided to get rid of Vassilissa for good. "I need a needle and thread to do some sewing," she said to Vassilissa. "Go and borrow some from my sister. She lives in the forest." The young girl trembled at the thought of going alone into the large, dark forest with its bears and wolves and who knows what.

Instead of going on her errand straightaway, Vassilissa went to see her real aunt, her mother's sister, to ask her advice. When Vassilissa explained what she had to do, her aunt turned pale; for the stepmother's sister was the evil witch Baba Yaga.

"My poor dear," said the aunt, "you must go. Your step-mother will punish you severely if you do not." She then gave Vassilissa some bread, ham, oil and a hair ribbon wrapped in a headscarf. "But take these with you," her aunt continued. "Your heart will tell you how to make best use of them."

Vassilissa couldn't understand what her aunt meant, but set off into the forest all the same on the path her stepmother had told her to take.

Eventually, Vassilissa arrived at Baba Yaga's house. It was a terrible place! The house stood on a gigantic pair of chicken legs; the garden around it was lit by the glowing eyes of skulls perched on sticks; the door was made of bones and the knocker was made of a set of jaws – wide open as if ready to bite! The poor child shook with fright.

Suddenly there was a great crash from the forest. It was Baba Yaga returning home. She travelled inside a huge magical mortar – easily big enough to grind human bones in. In one hand she held a large pestle which she hit against the ground to move about. In her other hand she carried a broom.

"What do you want? Why are you here?" asked Baba Yaga in her shrill, sour voice.

"Your sister – my stepmother – sent me to fetch a needle and thread," stammered Vassilissa in reply.

Now Baba Yaga knew immediately what her evil sister really wanted. She called for her maidservant and ordered her to set a big pot of water to heat over the fire. "It looks like I'll be dining on young girl tonight," whispered Baba Yaga to her servant.

Seeing the poor maidservant hard at work, all dressed in rags, tugged at Vassilissa's heart. She opened her parcel and offered the headscarf to the woman. The maidservant was so touched by the gift that she explained to Vassilissa what Baba Yaga planned to do.

Suddenly a black cat slunk into the room. He was so thin that his ribs were poking through his fur. This made Vassilissa's heart weep. From her parcel, she pulled out the ham and gave it to the cat. The cat's eyes opened wide in delight and he devoured the ham in seconds. The cat was so grateful that he told Vassilissa that he would help her escape.

"But how will I get away?" asked Vassilissa. "Baba Yaga will catch me in her magic mortar."

"Keep your ear to the ground," said the cat. "When you hear the thump of her pestle as she follows you, throw this towel behind you. A river will spring up and stop her. If Baba Yaga manages to find a way over it, drop this comb and an impassable forest will block her way."

The cat went off to distract Baba Yaga's attention while Vassilissa slipped out of the door. She had barely stepped outside when she was surrounded by three vicious-looking dogs. They looked half-starved and ready to eat Vassilissa without a second thought. But Vassilissa's heart went out to those poor famished hounds, and she gave them her aunt's bread. The dogs were touched by such tenderness and promptly allowed Vassilissa to pass by unharmed.

However, this was not the end of Vassilissa's problems. Now the garden gate started swinging violently backwards and forwards, making a loud squeaking noise which Baba Yaga would be sure to hear. Quick as a flash, Vassilissa poured some oil on the gate hinges. "Ooh," said the gate, "that feels better." And it opened to let Vassilissa out.

Now even the forest seemed to block her way, as the tree branches curved like claws to stop her. Vassilissa's heart told her to tie her ribbon to a branch. Immediately the branches parted to let her through.

Meanwhile, back in the house Baba Yaga was calling for Vassilissa: "Where are you, niece? It's time for dinner!"

The cat hid in the furthest part of the house and shouted out in his best little girl's voice: "I'm over here, my aunt."

No one could fool Baba Yaga for long though. She knew that the voice wasn't Vassilissa's. She grabbed the cat shouting: "You miserable animal, why have you betrayed me?"

The cat cried out as the evil witch beat him. "This is why I betrayed you!" he shouted. "She was the only person who has ever shown me any kindness. I hope she escapes!" And with that the cat bolted out of the window and Baba Yaga was left fuming in the room.

She spun on her heel and stormed out of the door. She was expecting to see the dogs all bloody around the mouth after eating Vassilissa, so when she saw them sleeping contentedly on the ground she was furious! She rained blows on the dogs screaming "Why, you traitors! Why have you betrayed me, too?"

"Traitors?" the dogs shouted back. "When have we ever let you down? And for what, some scraps of mouldy bread and blows from your evil hand? That girl fed us fresh bread and for her kindness we let her go. And good luck to her!"

Furious, Baba Yaga stomped to the gate and gave it a mighty kick. "You," she screamed. "What's your excuse for letting me down?"

"Letting you down?" replied the gate. "For years I've hung here, suffering as my hinges grated and you did nothing. For the price of some kindness and some oil I let her go free."

"They've all gone mad!" thought Baba Yaga. She leapt into her mortar, struck her pestle on the ground and was on her way. As she went, Baba Yaga called out to a tree, "Why are you wearing that stupid ribbon? You should have been stopping the girl!"

The tree replied like all the others before him, "I have been at your service since time began and you have done nothing for me. Yet the first time I meet the girl she gives me a gift. That's why I parted my branches and let her escape."

This sent Baba Yaga into even more of a fury and she doubled her efforts to catch Vassilissa. "This girl has been nothing but trouble," wailed the evil witch. "I'll make sure she never bothers me again!"

Vassilissa had been running as fast as her legs could carry her – but little girls' legs are no match for a witch. Sure enough, Vassilissa soon heard the thump, thump, thump, of Baba Yaga's mortar getting nearer. Then out of the trees flew the witch with her pointed teeth, wild hair and blazing eyes.

Immediately Vassilissa threw down the towel as the cat had told her to do. A huge, swirling river appeared, blocking Baba Yaga's way. The witch was not to be outdone, though. As Vassilissa ran, Baba Yaga commanded her bulls to come to her aid. These mighty beasts soon drank the river dry and the chase continued.

Vassilissa could hear Baba Yaga getting closer, so she tried her last chance of escape. She took the comb that the cat had given her and threw it to the ground. Immediately the teeth of the comb began to multiply and grow. Soon they had become a deep, impenetrable forest, with spiky branches so close together that even a mouse couldn't have squeezed through. Baba Yaga pulled and bit at the branches but it was no use, they were too thick and too many. Eventually she gave up and returned to her house on chicken legs and forgot about the little girl. In the meantime, Vassilissa sped home as fast as she could.

She ran straight into her father just as he was returning from the city. Before her stepmother could appear, she told him all about the errand she had been sent on and the witch and the cat, and dogs and forest and all the other terrors of the day.

Her father saw at once that he had made a huge mistake when he married his new wife, and banished her from the house. From that day on Vassilissa and her father lived in perfect happiness. As for Baba Yaga? Well, no one really knows. Bears or wolves may have eaten her. Or she may still be in the forest today.

THE FIRE BIRD AND THE GREY WOLF

Long ago, when kings ruled Russia, there was a Tsar who had three sons called Dimitri, Vassili and Ivan. This tsar owned a magnificent garden, and in that garden grew a tree which produced apples made of gold. However the tsar was troubled, for each night a mysterious robber was stealing these apples. He called his sons to him for help. "My boys, if any one of you can catch this criminal, I will give him half my kingdom."

The first night, the oldest of the brothers, Dimitri, stood guard over the golden apple tree. The night was long and soon Dimitri had fallen asleep, as did Vassili when he tried the next night. Then came the turn of Ivan, the youngest son of the Tsar, to keep watch over the tree. The night dragged on and though his eyelids grew heavy, he stayed awake.

Suddenly the garden was lit as if by a hundred suns: a bird with golden, sparkling feathers and crystal-bright eyes landed on the apple tree and started to take an apple. Ivan crept up to the bird, slowly, slowly … and jumped! He caught the bird by the tail but the bird flew off, leaving a solitary tail feather in the young man's hand.

The next morning Ivan went to the tsar.

"Father, I saw what has been stealing the apples. It was a great firebird – I tried to catch it, but all I could get was this." As he spoke, he took from his jacket the feather which he had put there for safekeeping. Instantly the room lit up as if by a thousand candles.

The bird never returned to steal the apples and the tsar rejoiced. However, over time, sadness seeped back into his life. He couldn't stop thinking of this most marvellous of birds – he had to have it! He called Dimitri and Vassili to him once more.

"My dearly beloved sons, saddle your horses and prepare for a journey. I want you to find the firebird and bring it back to me alive. I will give my kingdom to whoever succeeds."

The two brothers left together on their fastest horses. They were furious that Ivan had succeeded in plucking a feather from the firebird and were determined that he would not inherit the kingdom in their place.

The tsar was reluctant to let his youngest son go on such an arduous

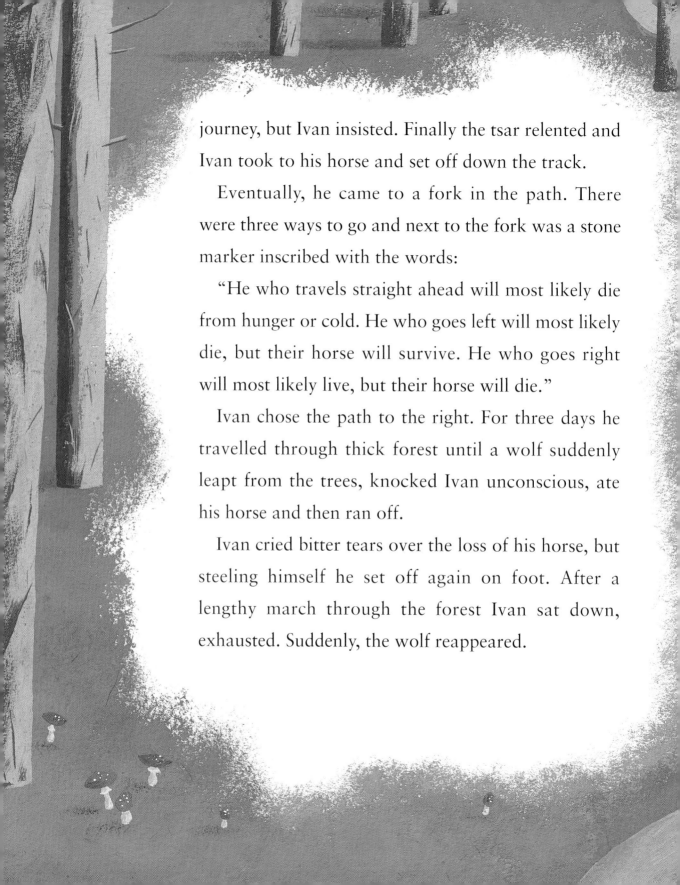

journey, but Ivan insisted. Finally the tsar relented and Ivan took to his horse and set off down the track.

Eventually, he came to a fork in the path. There were three ways to go and next to the fork was a stone marker inscribed with the words:

"He who travels straight ahead will most likely die from hunger or cold. He who goes left will most likely die, but their horse will survive. He who goes right will most likely live, but their horse will die."

Ivan chose the path to the right. For three days he travelled through thick forest until a wolf suddenly leapt from the trees, knocked Ivan unconscious, ate his horse and then ran off.

Ivan cried bitter tears over the loss of his horse, but steeling himself he set off again on foot. After a lengthy march through the forest Ivan sat down, exhausted. Suddenly, the wolf reappeared.

"Good evening, Prince Ivan," said the wolf, "I apologise for eating your horse, but you knew what would happen when you took the right-hand path. However, I feel sorry for you and will help. Climb on my back and I will take you on paths no horse could ever travel on."

Ivan sat on the wolf's back and said: "Take me to the firebird." The wolf set off, as swift as the wind, through the forest, past lakes, and over tundra.

The wolf ran for many days until he reached a land far to the north. He came to a halt next to a stone wall. "It is here, Ivan. Climb the wall and you will see a garden. Within this garden you will find a golden cage, and within this cage you will find the firebird. Take the bird if you wish, but take care not to touch the cage. Remember my words Ivan, or great ill will befall you."

Ivan climbed the wall, crossed the garden and found the cage and the magnificent bird. "I'll never get the firebird home without its cage," thought Ivan, "it will just fly off." So ignoring the wise words of the wolf, he reached out and grabbed the cage. Immediately bells rang and horns sounded and Ivan was surrounded by guards. They took him straight to their tsar – Dalmat the Terrible.

Red with rage, the tsar asked: "Who do you think you are, trying to steal my firebird?"

"I am Prince Ivan, son of Tsar Berendi," replied the young man. "My father requested that I bring him the firebird, for it had been stealing his golden apples."

"If you had asked my permission I would have gladly given you the bird," said Dalmat. "However, as you chose to try to steal it away from me, I shall treat you like a robber … unless you complete a task for me.

At the far end of the country, almost at the end of the world, lives Tsar Afron. He owns a horse with a golden mane. If you bring this marvellous animal to me, then I shall let you leave with your life and the firebird."

Reluctantly, Ivan agreed to do as the Tsar asked. Ivan sought out the grey wolf to tell him what had happened.

"I told you not to touch the cage!" cried the wolf. "Why did you not listen, Ivan?"

"I'm sorry, Grey Wolf," replied Ivan, crestfallen.

"Fine, fine," grumbled the wolf. "I will still help you. Now up onto my back, and let us find this horse with the golden mane."

Again the prince sat on the wolf's back, which then sped as fast as the wind in the direction of Afron's palace. Ivan and the wolf arrived outside the royal stables a few days later, cloaked in the dark of the night.

"Everyone sleeps," said the wolf. "Ivan, go now into the stable and get the horse with the golden mane. Whatever you do, don't touch his golden reins or bad luck will be sure to follow you."

Ivan crept into the stables and started to lead out the horse with the golden mane. Then he saw the golden reins hanging on the wall. "How can I take the horse all the way back to Tsar Dalmat without its sparkling reins?" Ignoring the wise words of the wolf, he unhooked the reins from the wall. Immediately bells rang and horns sounded and Ivan was surrounded by guards. They took him straight to Tsar Afron.

"Who are you that tries to steal my precious horse?" demanded Afron.

"I am Prince Ivan, son of Tsar Berendi," replied the young man.

"Such shame on you!" said the Tsar. "You, the son of a tsar, acting like a common criminal. If you had asked I would have given you the horse. Instead you tried to steal it, so I must treat you like a robber … unless you complete a task for me. At the bottom of the country lives the princess Helena the Beautiful. If you bring her to me I will spare your life and give you the horse with the golden mane."

In tears, Ivan sought the grey wolf and told him what had happened.

"Oh, I told you not to touch the reins!" exclaimed the wolf. "Do you ever listen? Well there's no point crying over spilt milk."

"I'm sorry, I really am," replied the prince.

"I'll forgive you this time," said the wolf. "Now stop snivelling, there's work to be done. Up, up, on my back. Let us find Helena the Beautiful and bring an end to all this."

Ivan climbed upon the grey wolf's back and they sped off as fast as the wind.

They eventually arrived at the bottom of the country and stopped by a golden gate.

"Prince Ivan, leave it to me now," said the wolf. "Wait for my return under the oak in the middle of the field."

The wolf left and found a hiding place, where he waited for Helena the Beautiful. As she walked past, the grey wolf leapt out, threw the girl upon his back and raced back to Prince Ivan who was waiting under the oak tree as instructed.

"Quick, Prince Ivan," cried the wolf as he approached. "Jump on my back!"

The prince joined Helena on the back of the wolf, who then sped across the country as fast as the wind itself. On their way back to Afron's palace Ivan and Helena fell in love, and the time for their separation came all too quickly. The young prince broke down in tears.

"Why are you so sad?" asked the wolf.

"Wolf," replied Ivan, "I am in love. Helena is the girl of my dreams. I could never – never! – give her up for a horse with a golden mane. But if I don't then I shall be killed."

"I have already given you a great deal of help," said the wolf, "but as your love is so strong I shall help you again. We shall hide Helena; I will take her form and accompany you to the palace. Afron will give you the horse with the golden mane as agreed. Take it, meet up with Helena and head for Dalmat's palace. I will catch up with you later."

The wolf somersaulted backwards and when he stood up he was the mirror image of Helena. Everything happened as the wolf predicted – the tsar gave Ivan the horse in exchange for the beautiful girl.

But when Tsar Afron married Helena he was not expecting to see the muzzle of a wolf in his bed instead of his bride. He sat petrified with fear as the wolf escaped. The wolf soon caught up with Ivan, his princess and the magnificent horse with the golden mane.

On they galloped for many days towards Dalmat's palace. As they approached the tsar's home Ivan broke down in tears again:

"Oh such sorrow! Now I must give up this magnificent horse for the firebird. Grey Wolf, my faithful friend, you have helped so much but I ask for one more favour."

He did not have to say any more, for the wolf understood perfectly.

"Of course," said the wolf. "Leave the horse here with Helena. I shall transform myself into a horse with a golden mane and you can take me to Dalmat. He will give you the firebird as your reward. Come back here and I will join you later."

The wolf did a somersault and turned into a horse with a golden mane. All that the wolf said came to pass. The tsar was overjoyed to see Ivan arriving with the

magnificent horse and he gave Ivan that which had
been promised: the firebird in the golden cage. But
that evening, when the tsar took his new steed out for
a gallop across the plains, the horse bucked and threw
him to the ground. No sooner had the tsar hit the dirt,
than the horse changed into a wolf and ran away.

The grey wolf met up again with Ivan and Helena and they continued on their journey home. Eventually they arrived at the place where the grey wolf had first eaten Ivan's horse. The wolf stopped and said:

"Prince Ivan, our ways separate here. Since we met at this spot I have helped you to find the firebird, the horse with the golden mane and Princess Helena the Beautiful. Please consider my help as a gift. Goodbye."

The grey wolf disappeared into the forest. Ivan turned the horse home and headed off towards his kingdom. After a while they needed to rest. Ivan tied his horse to a tree, hung the cage on a branch, then lay on the grass with his love Helena.

They were so deeply asleep that they did not hear the sound of people approaching. By a terrible coincidence it was Ivan's older brothers, Dimitri and Vassili. They had been searching all this time for the firebird and were returning home empty-handed and miserable.

"Look Dimitri!" said Vassili. "It is Ivan asleep on the grass. And look what he has found. Helena the Beautiful, the firebird and the horse with the golden mane! Our father will surely give him the kingdom, and we, his elders, will be left with nothing!"

Consumed with jealousy and rage, the brothers vowed to kill their sibling and steal his treasures. Dimitri drove his sword through Ivan's sleeping body. Helena woke and burst into tears. Vassili grabbed her roughly and pressed the point of his sword against her throat:

"You will be marrying me now, my pretty one – or end up dead like young Ivan. And don't even think about telling our father what you saw!"

Then the brothers collected the treasures and set off to the palace. They left the body of their brother for the crows and wolves.

Thirty days later, the grey wolf passed by the body of Ivan. Recognising the prince, the wolf tried to resuscitate him, but could not do it – only magic would help now. Seeing a mother crow approaching the body, the wolf ran off to her nest and took one of her young and held it in his jaws.

"Listen, mother crow," said the wolf, "if you want to see your baby alive again you must complete a task for me. Fly across the steppes, the mountains, forests and lakes and find me the waters of life and death."

The crow, spurred on by fear, flew to the ends of the earth and back within three days, bringing back two bottles of water. The wolf poured the water of the dead on Prince Ivan and his wounds were healed.

Then he poured the water of life on Ivan and the young man immediately sat up and said:

"Ah, what a fantastic sleep!"

"Yes, Prince Ivan," said the wolf. "Without me you slept so well you did not wake when your brothers murdered you and took off with the firebird, the horse with the golden mane and Helena the Beautiful. And today Vassili is about to marry Helena. Quick, on my back if you want to stop this wedding."

Ivan leapt upon the wolf's back and they sped off even faster than the wind. When they arrived at the palace, Ivan thanked his friend and charged into the palace chapel. The wedding had just started. Helena, seeing Ivan threw her arms around him, crying out, "Ivan can it be true? My fiancé who found the firebird and the horse with the golden mane, and whose brothers are robbers and assassins!"

The tsar made Helena explain what she meant. On hearing the truth, he flung the older brothers into the deepest dungeon in the palace and never spoke of them again. Ivan and Helena were married with the grey wolf as guest of honour and lived happily for many years, never knowing the shadow of sadness to fall upon their door.